States OHIO

by Tyler Maine

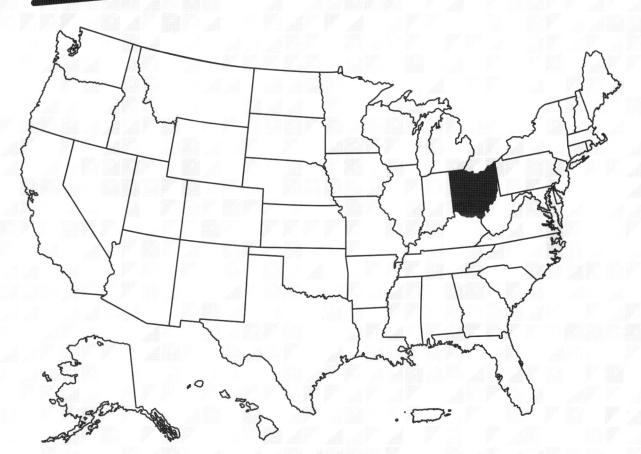

CAPSTONE PRESS
a capstone imprint

Next Page Books are published by Capstone Press,
1710 Roe Crest Drive, North Mankato, Minnesota 56003
www.mycapstone.com

Library of Congress Cataloging-in-Publication Data
Cataloging-in-publication information is on file with the Library of
Congress.
ISBN 978-1-5157-0422-5 (library binding)
ISBN 978-1-5157-0481-2 (paperback)
ISBN 978-1-5157-0533-8 (ebook PDF)

Editorial Credits
Jaclyn Jaycox, editor; Richard Korab and Katy LaVigne, designers;
Morgan Walters, media researcher; Tori Abraham, production specialist

Photo Credits
Capstone Press: Angi Gahler, map 4, 7; Dreamstime: Adeliepenguin, 11,
Jeders2, 9; iStockphoto: JanelleStreed, top left 20; Library of Congress:
Prints and Photographs Division, middle 18, Emil P. Spahn, bottom 18,
28; NASA, top 18; Newscom: Everett Collection, 29, ZUMAPRESS/Nancy
Kaszerman, bottom 19; North Wind Picture Archives, 12, 25; One Mile
Up, Inc., flag, seal 23; Shutterstock: aceshot1, 16, 17, Adam Derewecki,
bottom 24, Aleksei Verhovski, top right 20, Connie Barr, bottom left 20,
Denis Tabler, bottom left 21, Domenic Gareri, middle 19, Doug Lemke,
bottom right 8, Everett Historical, 26, Featureflash, top 19, Georgios
Kollidas, 27, Joseph Sohm, 6, 10, 15, Kenneth Sponsler, 5, LehaKoK,
bottom right 20, Michael Richardson, bottom right 21, Muskoka Stock
Photos, middle left 21, Nagel Photography, 13, Narong Jongsirikul,
top 24, Ross Ellet, bottom left 8, Rudy Balasko, cover, sarsmis, 14, SF
photo, 7, StockPhotosLV, top right 21, Tom Reichner, middle right 21,
wiktord, top left 21

All design elements by Shutterstock

Printed and bound in China.
0316/CA21600187
012016 009436F16

TABLE OF CONTENTS

Want to take your research further? Ask your librarian if your school subscribes to PebbleGo Next. If so, when you see this helpful symbol ⬆ throughout the book, log onto www.pebblegonext.com for bonus downloads and information.

LOCATION

Ohio is one of the nation's midwestern states. It lies between Indiana on the west and Pennsylvania on the east. To the south is Kentucky. West Virginia curls around Ohio's southeastern corner. Michigan borders the northwest. Lake Erie, one of North America's five Great Lakes, lies north of Ohio. Ohio's capital and largest city is Columbus. Cleveland and Cincinnati are the state's next largest cities.

PebbleGo Next Bonus!
To print and label
your own map, go to
www.pebblegonext.com
and search keywords:
OH MAP

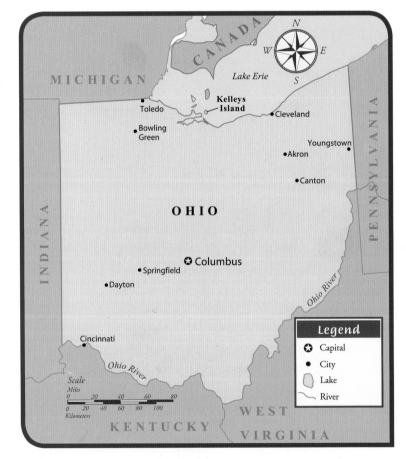

Cleveland was named for Revolutionary War soldier, Moses Cleaveland, in 1796. A local newspaper misspelled the name and it stuck.

GEOGRAPHY

Ohio is made up of lowlands and plateaus. The state's lowest elevation is 455 feet (139 meters) above sea level. This occurs in the south along the Ohio River. Much of Ohio's land is flat plains that were once the bottom of Lake Erie. Some low ridges called moraines sit in western Ohio. Campbell Hill, the state's highest point, is in this area. It rises 1,549 feet (472 m) above sea level.

PebbleGo Next Bonus! To watch a video about the Wright Brothers, go to www.pebblegonext.com and search keywords:

OH VIDEO

The Scioto River is one of Ohio's longest rivers at more than 200 miles (320 kilometers) long.

Located just north of Ohio, South Bass Island is surrounded by the waters of Lake Erie.

Lake Erie

Maumee River

Sandusky River

Cuyahoga Valley National Park

CENTRAL LOWLAND

Scioto River

APPALACHIAN PLATEAUS

Campbell Hill

Great Miami River

Muskingum River

Ohio River

Ohio River

INTERIOR LOW PLATEAU

Scale
Miles
0   20   40   60   80
0   20   40   60   80   100
Kilometers

Legend
▲ Highest Point
■ Park
〜 River
◯ Lake

WEATHER

Ohio's central U.S. location makes for warm summers and cool winters. The average summer temperature in Ohio is 71 degrees Fahrenheit (22 degrees Celsius). The average winter temperature is 29°F (-2°C).

Average High and Low Temperatures (Columbus, OH)

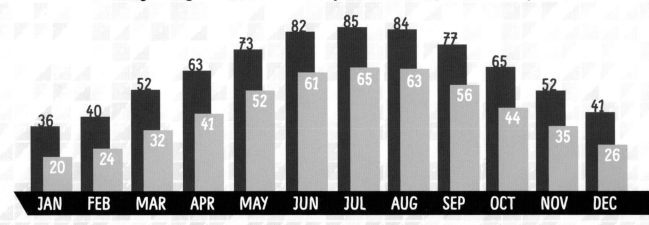

	JAN	FEB	MAR	APR	MAY	JUN	JUL	AUG	SEP	OCT	NOV	DEC
High	36	40	52	63	73	82	85	84	77	65	52	41
Low	20	24	32	41	52	61	65	63	56	44	35	26

LANDMARKS

Serpent Mound

Adams County displays a large snake-shaped mound built by ancient Ohio natives. It is the largest of its kind in the United States.

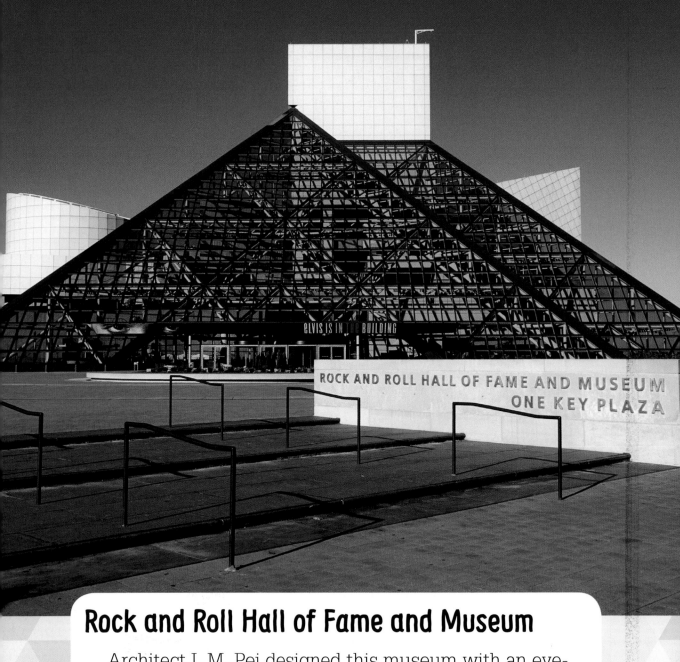

Rock and Roll Hall of Fame and Museum

Architect I. M. Pei designed this museum with an eye-catching glass pyramid. The museum's collection includes items from The Beatles, Elvis Presley, Michael Jackson, and other rock and roll stars.

Cedar Point Amusement Park

Often called the roller coaster capital, Cedar Point amusement park has 16 roller coasters and many other thrill rides. It is located near Lake Erie in Sandusky.

Rufus Putnam (1738–1824) was an American Revolutionary soldier who founded Ohio's first white settlement, Marietta.

Although native people have lived in Ohio for thousands of years, French explorer René Robert Cavelier, known as Sieur de La Salle, first arrived around 1670. After the French and Indian wars (1689–1763), Ohio became a British territory until the end of the Revolutionary War (1775–1783). Ohio became part of the Northwest Territory in 1787. Pioneers from eastern states started the first white settlement, Marietta, in 1788. Ohio became the 17th state in 1803.

Ohio's state government has three branches. The governor heads the executive branch. The legislature is called the General Assembly. It is made up of the Senate with 33 members and the House of Representatives with 99 members. The General Assembly makes the laws. The judicial branch is made up of several judges who uphold the laws.

Ohio's capitol building took 22 years to be completed.

INDUSTRY

Ohio is a leading agricultural and industrial state. Ohio is a leader in producing rubber, plastics, stone, clay, and glass products. The state's rivers make it easy to quickly transport goods.

Ohio's geography and natural resources also shape its industry. Its rich soil and good climate are great for growing crops. The two main crops in Ohio are corn and soybeans. Ohio is a top-ten state for growing apples. Ohio is also a big producer of tomatoes. Livestock and eggs also contribute to the state's economy.

Apples have been important to the state since the pioneer days. Johnny Appleseed planted many orchards throughout the state.

Barges transporting cargo are a common site on the Ohio River.

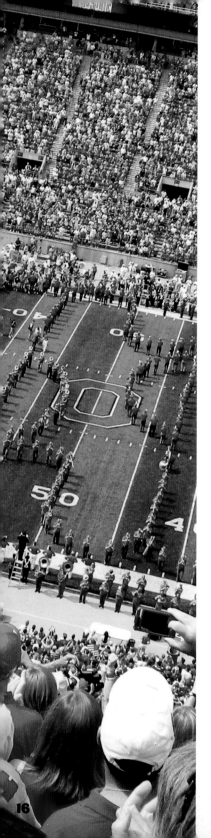

POPULATION

Many settlers came to Ohio from European countries. English and Scottish-Irish people first settled the area. Later people from all around Europe came, attracted by Ohio's resources. Some came to Ohio to find jobs and some came to farm the land.

Others, like Jewish and Amish people, wanted to freely practice their religions. Ohio's Holmes County has the largest Amish population in the world. Amish people live simple lives. They do not use cars or electricity.

Population by Ethnicity

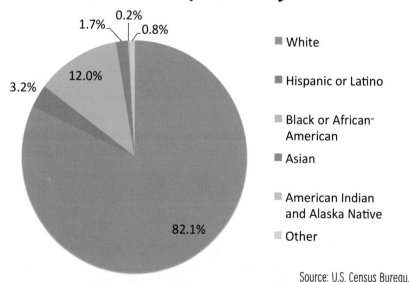

- 0.2%
- 1.7%
- 0.8%
- 12.0%
- 3.2%
- 82.1%

- White
- Hispanic or Latino
- Black or African-American
- Asian
- American Indian and Alaska Native
- Other

Source: U.S. Census Bureau.

African-Americans have been living in Ohio for hundreds of years. The Underground Railroad, which was a system that helped slaves in the South reach freedom in the North during the mid-1800s, brought many of the first African-American residents to the state.

Other groups continue to move to Ohio because of its many jobs. Ohio no longer has any Indian reservations, which makes its American Indian population very small.

FAMOUS PEOPLE

John Glenn (1921–) is the first American to orbit Earth. He was part of the *Mercury 7* astronaut program. He returned to space in 1998 and became the oldest person to fly in space at age 77. He was also a U.S. senator for more than 20 years. He was born in Cambridge.

Ulysses S. Grant (1822–1885) was a famous general in the American Civil War and became the 18th president. He was born in Point Pleasant.

Thomas Edison (1847–1931) was a famous inventor. He is known for his work on lightbulbs, phonographs, and motion picture cameras. He was born in Milan.

Drew Carey (1958–) is a game show host, TV personality, and comedian. He has been the host of *The Price is Right* since 2007. He was born in Cleveland.

LeBron James (1984–) is a star basketball player. He played several seasons for the Cleveland Cavaliers before becoming a member of the Miami Heat. In 2014 he returned to play for the Cavaliers. He has won four NBA Most Valuable Player Awards and two Olympic gold medals, among other awards. He was born in Akron.

R. L. Stine (1943–) is a children's author who writes scary stories. His books have sold more than 400 million copies. He was born in Columbus.

STATE SYMBOLS

Tree

Ohio buckeye

Flower

scarlet carnation

Bird

cardinal

Fossil

trilobite

PebbleGo Next Bonus! To make a dessert using one of Ohio's top-produced fruits, go to www.pebblegonext.com and search keywords: **OH RECIPE**

Gemstone

flint

Fruit

tomato

Wildflower

large white trillium

Animal

white-tailed deer

Insect

ladybug

Reptile

black racer snake

FAST FACTS

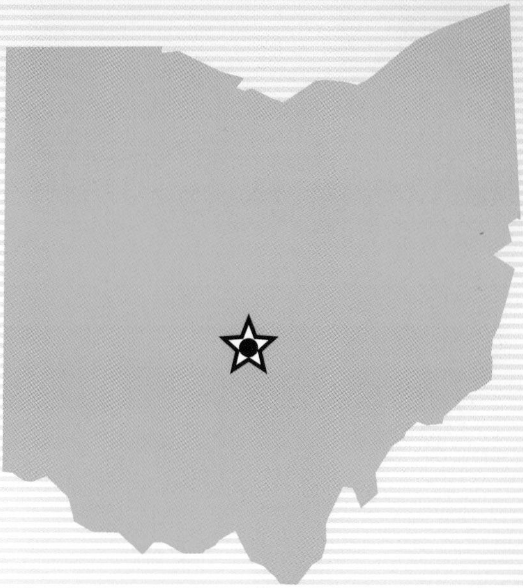

STATEHOOD
1803

CAPITAL ☆
Columbus

LARGEST CITY •
Columbus

SIZE
40,861 square miles (105,830 square kilometers)
land area (2010 U.S. Census Bureau)

POPULATION
11,570,808 (2013 U.S. Census estimate)

STATE NICKNAME
Buckeye State

STATE MOTTO
"With God, all things are possible"

STATE SEAL

The Great Seal of Ohio has been around for hundreds of years. Pictures in the seal show important symbols to Ohio. The bundle of wheat stands for Ohio's agricultural strength. A bundle of 17 arrows shows that Ohio was the 17th state. The sun rising over Mount Logan shows that Ohio was the first state west of the Allegheny Mountains.

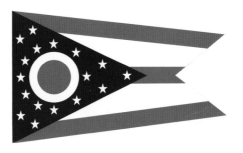

**PebbleGo Next Bonus!
To print and color
your own flag, go to
www.pebblegonext.com
and search keywords:
OH FLAG**

STATE FLAG

Ohio's flag was adopted in 1902. It has the shape of a bird's tail. It is called a burgee shape. A triangle and circle make up most of the design. The triangle shape stands for Ohio's hills and valleys. The white circle with a red center on top of the triangle forms the letter "O" for Ohio. It also looks like a Buckeye nut. The Buckeye is the state tree of Ohio and residents are known as Buckeyes. Red and white stripes flow across the flag like the state's waterways and roads. The 17 stars show that Ohio is the 17th state.

MINING PRODUCTS

coal, limestone, natural gas

MANUFACTURED GOODS

chemicals, fabricated metals, food products, petroleum and coal products, motor vehicles and parts

FARM PRODUCTS

soybeans, corn, wheat, tomatoes, cattle, poultry, hogs, eggs

PebbleGo Next Bonus! To learn the lyrics to the state song, go to www.pebblegonext.com and search keywords: **OH SONG**

PROFESSIONAL SPORTS TEAMS

Cincinnati Bengals (NFL)
Cleveland Browns (NFL)
Cincinnati Reds (MLB)
Cleveland Indians (MLB)
Cleveland Cavaliers (NBA)
Columbus Blue Jackets (NHL)
Columbus Crew (MLS)

OHIO TIMELINE

100 BC
The Hopewell people join the Adena people in Ohio. Proof of their mound-building cultures can still be seen.

AD 1620
The Pilgrims establish a colony in the New World in present-day Massachusetts.

1650
The Iroquois drive other groups out of Ohio.

1670
French explorer René Robert Cavelier, known as Sieur de la Salle, explores the Ohio River.

1788
Rufus Putnam and the Ohio Company found Marietta, the first white settlement.

1803 Ohio becomes the 17th state on March 1.

1812–1814 Ohio's location plays a key role in the War of 1812. This war between the United States and Great Britain has a famous battle on Lake Erie.

1825 Ohio begins to build canals.

1841 Ohio resident William Henry Harrison becomes the 9th president on March 4.

1861–1865
The Union and the Confederacy fight the Civil War. Ohio fights with the Union.

1869
Ohioan Ulysses S. Grant becomes the 18th president on March 4.

1877
Ohio-born Rutherford B. Hayes becomes the 19th president on March 4.

1881
After serving nine consecutive terms in the U.S. House of Representatives, Ohio congressman James A. Garfield becomes the 20th president.

1889
Benjamin Harrison from North Bend becomes the 23rd president.

1897 Former Ohio governor William McKinley becomes the 25th president on March 4.

1909 William H. Taft becomes the 7th Ohioan to be president. He becomes the 27th president on March 4.

1914–1918 World War I is fought; the United States enters the war in 1917.

1921 Ohio senator Warren G. Harding becomes the 29th president on March 4.

1939–1945 World War II is fought; the United States enters the war in 1941.

1970

On May 4 the Ohio National Guard fires into a crowd of protesters at Kent State. Four students are killed and nine others are injured.

2008

Ohio manufacturing cities like Cleveland hit hard times during the Great Recession (December 2007–June 2009). Many jobs are lost and people begin moving away. In 2008 the government loans money to automakers and Ohio's economy begins to recover.

2012

The city of Columbus celebrates its 200th anniversary.

2015

In June, the Intelligent Community Forum names Columbus the smartest city in the world. The mayor is presented with the 2015 Intelligent Community of the Year award.

Glossary

executive *(ig-ZE-kyuh-tiv)*—the branch of government that makes sure laws are followed

industry *(IN-duh-stree)*—a business which produces a product or provides a service

judicial *(joo-DISH-uhl)*—to do with the branch of government that explains and interprets the laws

legislature *(LEJ-iss-lay-chur)*—a group of elected officials who have the power to make or change laws for a country or state

moraine *(MOOR-ayn)*—mounds of earth and stones left by a melting glacier

natural resource *(NACH-ur-uhl REE-sorss)*—a material found in nature that is useful to people

petroleum *(puh-TROH-lee-uhm)*—an oily liquid found below the earth's surface used to make gasoline, heating oil, and many other products

phonograph *(FOH-nuh-graf)*—a machine that plays sounds that have been recorded in the grooves of a record; a record has recorded sound or music

plateau *(pla-TOH)*—an area of high, flat land

pyramid *(PIHR-uh-mid)*—a solid building with sloping sides that come together at the top

transport *(transs-PORT)*—to move or carry something or someone from one place to another

Read More

Bailer, Darice. *What's Great About Ohio?* Our Great States. Minneapolis: Lerner Publications, 2016.

Ganeri, Anita. *United States of America: A Benjamin Blog and His Inquisitive Dog Guide.* Country Guides. Chicago: Heinemann Raintree, 2015.

Hart, Joyce. *Ohio.* It's My State! New York: Marshall Cavendish Benchmark, 2012.

Internet Sites

FactHound offers a safe, fun way to find Internet sites related to this book. All of the sites on FactHound have been researched by our staff.

Here's all you do:

Visit *www.facthound.com*

Type in this code: 9781515704225

 Check out projects, games and lots more at
www.capstonekids.com

Critical Thinking Using the Common Core

1. Which of the five Great Lakes touches Ohio? (Key Ideas and Details)

2. Look at the pie chart on page 16. What percentage of Ohio's population is white? (Craft and Structure)

3. Thomas Edison is known for his work on lightbulbs, phonographs, and motion picture cameras. What is a phonograph? (Craft and Structure)

Index